Pearl

VERSES THE

World

Pearl
VERSES THE
World

SALLY MURPHY

illustrated by
HEATHER POTTER

CANDLEWICK PRESS

First U.S. edition 2011

Library of Congress Cataloging-in-Publication Data
Murphy, Sally.
Pearl verses the world / Sally Murphy ; [illustrations by Heather Potter]. — 1st U.S. ed.
p. cm.
Summary: Pearl feels like an island in school, isolated and alone, but at home she feels
loved and secure until her grandmother's illness changes the way Pearl views her world.
ISBN 978-0-7636-4821-3
[1. Loneliness — Fiction. 2. Family life — Fiction. 3. Grandmothers — Fiction.
4. Schools — Fiction. 5. Poetry — Fiction. 6. Death — Fiction.]
I. Potter, Heather, ill. II. Title.
PZ7.M9552Pe 2011
[Fic] — dc22   2010040149

11 12 13 14 15 16 BVG 10 9 8 7 6 5 4 3 2 1

Printed in Berryville, VA, U.S.A.

This book was typeset in Scala.
The illustrations were done in pencil and ink.

Candlewick Press
99 Dover Street
Somerville, Massachusetts 02144

visit us at www.candlewick.com

For Grandma, Garmie,
and Grandma Chadd,
and for
grandmothers everywhere
S. M.

For my father, John Alfred Potter,
who was so proud of
all seven of us
H. P.

Sometimes I think
that I am on an island—
a deserted one
with just a single coconut tree.

Other days I think
I'm trapped in a bubble
floating aimlessly through a void.

Wherever I am
no one sees me.

My class is made up
of groups:
the sporty boys' group,
the ballet girls' group,
the library kids' group,
the bus kids' group,
the rough kids' group.

I am in a group of one.

Miss Bruff
teaches our class.
Every day she stands at the front
and tries to inspire us
with lessons about planets
and conservation
and the magic of math.
Her singsong voice
floats through the air—

It should encourage us,
fill us with hope
and with happiness.
But mostly, when it reaches us,
it thuds like concrete.

Mitchell Mason is scratching his knee,
Joseph Little is picking his nose,
Lucy Wong (who used to be my friend)
is planning a game of hopscotch
for recess.
And me?
I am thinking of home
and what is happening there.

Miss Bruff wants us to write poems.
I am.
Miss Bruff wants poems that rhyme.
Mine don't.
Rhyme is okay sometimes,
but my poems don't rhyme
and neither do I.

There was a young lady called Pearl
Who was not a rhyming type girl.
She said, "I've no time
For poems that rhyme,"
Which made her poor teacher go hurl.

There is no nicer noise
than the sound of the bell
at the end of the day.
One minute you are agonizing
over what word rhymes with *sausage*
or what is the answer to 11 times 12
and the next
you are released
by the *brrringing*
and *rrringing*
of the final bell.

And you know that no matter how hard
your day has been,
now it is over
and you can get out of here.
You try to stay still
while you say
Good afternoon, Miss Bruff.
But it is hard
and soon your legs are carrying you
away from the classroom
that has been your prison
for the day
and home,
where you belong.

There are three people at our house:
me,
my mom,
and my granny.
And that is how it has been
for as long as I can remember.
Dad went away
before I was born.
His loss, Mom says.
I don't care.
How can I miss
someone I never knew?

But I know my granny
and Granny knows me.
That is why I miss her so much.
She is still here with us
but she doesn't remember who we are.
She lies in her room
sleeping, or drooling, or tossing wildly.

Granny is fading.
So are Mom and me.

Mom, I say.
Mmmmmm, she says.
She doesn't look up.
Nothing, I say.
She keeps reading.
I want to ask:
Will Granny get better?
Will she sit up and smile
when I enter the room?
Will she make me laugh
with her jokes about chickens and roads?
But Mom is tuned out.
She is reading,
shut in the world of her novel.
Perhaps things are happier
there in those pages.
Lucky Mom.
Maybe I should get a book, too.

My bookshelf is filled
with the books Granny bought me
when I was little.
Fairy tales, mostly.
I read.
There was once a little princess
who was trapped in a high tower
by a wicked witch
with a wart on her nose.
Miss Bruff is a wicked witch
but she does not have a wart on her nose.
I don't think.
Perhaps she does and she hides it
with all that makeup she wears to school.
Every day the princess sat at her window
waiting to be rescued by a handsome prince.
I wonder if the prince was as handsome
as Mitchell Mason.
He is very handsome
even though he is not a prince.
Just a boy in my class.
But I wonder,
Why does the prince need to be handsome?
I wonder if all princes
are supposed to be handsome.

And why does the princess
wait for the prince, anyway?
Why doesn't she do something about
rescuing herself?
She should be proactive.
That's what Mom would say
if she wasn't lost in her own book.
The princess sat, and while she sat she spun.
Spinning, spinning, spinning.
All day, spinning.

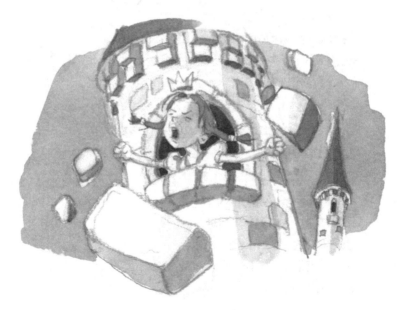

Spinning is fun
even when it makes you dizzy.
I like to stretch my arms out wide

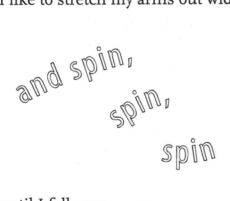

and spin,
spin,
spin

until I fall over.
Then I lie on the grass
and watch the clouds spinning above me.
But the princess doesn't seem
so big on spinning.
Maybe her kind of spinning isn't so fun.
I don't like this story.
Time for a new book.

At school Miss Bruff
is still wanting poems.
Good ones, she says.
With lots of rhyme
and rhythm.
Miss Bruff, I'd like to say,
there is no rhythm in me.
There is no rhythm in my life.
How can I write it down
on a page
when it isn't there?
But Miss Bruff is not
that kind of teacher.
So instead I write:

A teacher known as Bruff
Was very, very gruff.
She preached and she taught
Much more than she ought
Till the class had had more than enough.

I snicker.
Mitchell Mason looks over my shoulder
and reads what I've written.
He smiles.

My world is filled
with rhyme
just for a moment
until I see Miss Bruff coming down the aisle.
She will not smile when she sees my verse.
I crumple my poem into a tight ball
and I stare at a fresh, empty page,
waiting for new words to come.

On her way past my desk
Prudence Jones,
prettiest girl in the class,
most popular girl in the class,
most perfect girl in the class,
bumps my desk.
My pencils cascade
onto the floor.
Prudence! Miss Bruff gruffs.

Prudence's face
is a picture of innocence.
Sorry, Miss Bruff, she says.
It was an accident.
But down on the floor
as she passes me a pencil,
she nudges me and hisses,
That's for stealing my boyfriend.
Does Prudence have a boyfriend?
And how could I steal him
when I don't know who he is?
And would he let himself be stolen?

I sit back in my chair
and chew my pencil,
wondering who
this mysterious boyfriend could be
and what I would do with him
if I did steal him.
Then I see Prudence
glaring daggers at Mitchell Mason.

Roses are red;
Violets are blue.
No one glares harder
Than an angry Prue.

In the library
I search for a good book.
We have many books,
says Mrs. Rose, the librarian,
and ALL of them are good.
Of course she says that.
It's her job.
But do I want to read about
Trucks
Trains and
Transport?
Or even
Horses
Houses and
Hyenas?

In the fiction corner
there are pink books
full of princesses
and girls who want to be princesses
and black books
about bad boys
and brave boys
and brawny boys.

Where is the book
about a girl
whose poems don't rhyme
and whose Granny is fading?
Pearl, says Mrs. Rose,
the bell has rung.

I go back to class
empty-handed
empty-headed
empty-hearted.

On Tuesday afternoons
our class goes swimming.
I dive down
to the bottom of the pool,
blow bubbles,
and watch them

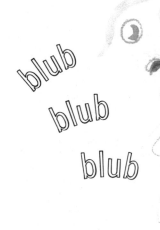

blub
blub
blub

to the surface.
It is quiet down there
in my cold cocoon
but soon I need air.
At the surface
I breathe deeply,
ready to submerge once more.

Pearl, says Ryan,
the swimming instructor,
you cannot learn to swim
on the bottom of the pool.
Stay up here
and listen to me.

I don't want
to learn to swim.
What I want
is a set of gills
so I can stay under
without drowning.

At the shallow end
some old ladies
are jumping
and lunging
and stretching.
Aquarobics.
They have pink swimming caps
and flowery suits
and happy smiles
on their faces.
Granny would love
aquarobics—
if only she
were not confined
to her little bed
in our little house.

At home
I talk to Granny,
tell her about
the aquarobics ladies.
You should see it, Granny.
I jump
and lunge
and stretch,
then fall down
laughing.
Granny does not laugh.
But just for a moment
her eyes meet mine
and I think she's in there.
If only
she could come out
to play.

Mom used to work
in the bank
up the road.
She says she will again
one day.
But since Granny got sick,
she's been on
compassionate leave.
My dictionary says
compassionate means pitying.
Who is pitying who?
Is the bank manager pitying Mom?
Is Mom pitying Granny?
Or is Mom pitying herself?
Sounds pitiful to me.
But I am glad
Mom can take time
to care for Granny.
I think Granny would be glad, too—
if she remembered who Mom was.

So Mom spends her days
and her nights
looking after her mom, my granny.
Wiping her nose, her brow, her bottom.

Never complaining
but always looking so tired.
So
very
tired.

While Mom cooks dinner,
I sit with Granny.
She is looking out the window.
I look, too, and remember
how Granny used to
push me on that swing,

how Granny and I
planted that rosebush,
how Granny and I
painted that old bench.
I sigh.
Something rolls down Granny's cheek.
A tear.
Does Granny remember, too?

I take her hand.
Her feathery skin is cool.
Her muscles don't respond.
But Granny is still in there somewhere.

When Granny sleeps,
Mom sits down with me.
Granny has to go away, she says.
The doctor wants her
to be looked after
in a home with other old people.
No! I cry.
She is ours.
She belongs here
with me
and with you.
We are all she needs.
Mom strokes my cheek.
Pearl, she sighs,
I love Granny, too.
But I cannot care for her
and neither can you.
But I do care.
I care and care and care.
And so does Mom.

We need Granny here with us,
and Granny needs to be with us
or she will die.
Pearl, says Mom,
Granny is going to die soon
even if she stays here.
I want to plug my ears.
I want to sing

la, la, LALALALALA

so loudly
that Mom's words are drowned.
But instead I swallow.
Yes, Mom,
but she should die with us,
not with strangers
who don't know how she was,
who she is.
Mom sighs.
We'll see, she says.
But I don't know
how much longer we can last—
you,
Granny,
and me.

There are three people at my house
and that's the way it should stay
forever:
me,
my mom,
and my granny.
If you take one away,
we won't be whole
anymore,
like a shoe without a lace
or a flower with no petals.
It takes three
to make our family,
never one or two.

Lying still in bed
is hard
when your head is broiling
and churning
with a gazillion thoughts.
How can I save Granny?
Mom cannot send her away.
How could she?
I remember
Mom and Granny
laughing together
in the kitchen,
working together
in the garden,
cheering together
at football
on TV.
Now they are two people:
Mom feeding Granny,
Mom washing Granny,
Mom worrying about Granny.

Through the velvety darkness
I hear a noise from Granny's room.
I creep down the hall.
I don't like what I see:
Mom's head in her hands,
crying softly
as she sits at Granny's side.

At school
the groups gather
waiting for the bell.
In my group of one
I sit on the bench
remembering last night,
thinking about my mom
and my granny.
But my group of one grows.
Mitchell Mason is next to me.
I liked your poem, he says.
Then he goes again,
leaving just a memory of his smile
and the sound of his voice.
A hiss
like an angry cat
comes from
the ballet group.
Prudence Jones is scowling.
She should be told
that when she does that
she's no longer
the prettiest girl in the class.

Today, says Miss Bruff,
you must write
about someone you know.
Remember those rhymes!
Miss B, I want to say,
some people don't rhyme,
and some of us
don't even want to rhyme.
Instead I chew my pencil
and look around the room.
Mitchell Mason chews, too.
Prudence Jones
writes perfect letters
on a perfect page.
She probably rhymes.
Perfectly.
She sees me looking
and glares.
Mitchell looks, too,
and Prudence smiles
smilingly.

I must write
or Miss Bruff
will go nuts.

There was a nice boy called Mitch
Whose girlfriend was a real —

Uh-oh.
I'd better not write that.

I'm not sure
that Prudence Jones
could really
be a . . . witch.
Even if she's not very nice.
Another piece of paper
is crumpled
and tossed into the bin.
Miss Bruff withers me
with her stare.

I try again,
holding my pencil tight,
willing the rhymes to come.

My teacher's name is Miss B.
She's as nice as nice can be,
But I don't think she'll ever see
Why rhyme is not the thing for me.

Bleh.
This poem is not for me, either.
I chew some more
and try again.

A cat
A rat
A bat
A hat
All rhyme —
Why, fancy that!
But life is not
All hats and cats
And sometimes rhyme
Just leaves me flat.

There.
I have written
a poem that rhymes.
Miss Bruff reads over my shoulder
and sighs.
Mitchell Mason
reads over my shoulder
and smiles.
At least somebody
is happy.

Mrs. Tiller, the principal,
lives in her office
coming out only to feed
on naughty boys
or silly girls
who attract her attention.
Sometimes she speaks
at assemblies:
blah blah lunchroom,
blah blah sports equipment,
blah blah awards,
blah blah blah.
But she has never before appeared
at our classroom door.

She comes in quietly.
A hush falls
as we all pretend to be working
but really we are watching
waiting
to see
who is in trouble.

She whispers to Miss Bruff,
who frowns and looks at me.
I try to turn back to my work
but the principal looks, too.
Pearl Barrett, she says,
May I see you, please?

My mind whirls
as I stand up.
What have I done wrong?
Prudence is smiling
sneeringly.
Perhaps she has told.
Is accidentally stealing
someone's boyfriend
a crime?

The principal's office
is not very cozy
but at least it is warmer
than the echoey hallway
we have just walked down.
She didn't speak to me,
just ushered me here, frowning.

I didn't want to talk, anyway.
What do you say
about a crime
you didn't mean to commit?

In my head
I prepare my defense.
I am sorry, Mrs. Tiller,
I will say.
I did not mean
to steal Prudence Jones's boyfriend.
I did not even know
that she had a boyfriend I could steal.
Besides which
I do not want a boyfriend,
even one as cute as Mitchell Mason
with dreamy eyes and a friendly smile.
I am a group of one.
If I had a boyfriend,
I might be a group of two.

Mrs. Tiller is looking at me strangely.
Did I say that out loud?

I don't think so—
my mouth is too dry to speak.
She he-hems a little.
Maybe hers is, too.
Pearl, she says at last,
I have some bad news.
Bad news?
Getting in trouble is always bad news.
But I look at her face
and suddenly I see
that I am not in trouble.
Mrs. Tiller's eyes are not angry.
They are sad.
Scared even.
Is she scared of me?

When Mrs. Tiller utters those words,
I run.
I run and run.
I want to be outside.
She calls my name
but inside my head
all I hear
is the echo of those words.
How could she say them?
Why did she say them?
Those words.
They can't be true.

On the playground
my favorite tree waits.
This tree reminds me of home.
It is old and sprawling
and comforting.
Many times
I have sat under this tree
at recess or lunch.
Mostly in my group of one.

Now I lie on my back
and stare up into the branches,
branches I can't see so well
through the water clouding my eyes.
The words are in my head.
I can hear Mrs. Tiller saying them
over
and over
and over.
Your granny has died.

Why would she say such a thing?

Miss Bruff appears,
speaking softly.
Come on, Pearl, she says.
I am taking you home.
Yes.
Home is good.
Home is where Mom is.
Home is where Granny is.
They will tell me
everything is okay.
They will laugh
when I tell them
about Mrs. Tiller's words.
But still my legs don't want
to lift me up
to make the walk
from the tree
to Miss Bruff's car.

Mom opens the door
and I see her eyes,
sadder than sad can be.
And I don't need to ask
if it's true.
Granny has died.
She has gone away
just like Mom wanted.
I want to yell at Mom
and remind her of the things
she said last night.
But her eyes are so sad
and I remember
her tears in the dark.

At the funeral home
there are many books.
They have big titles and
make big promises:
Coping with Grief,
Moving On,
Healing after Loss.
There is even a book
for kids called
Good-bye, Grandad.
I want to kick at the shelf,
pull out the books,
and tear out their pages.

Mom and Charles
(our "personal funeral planner")
talk about caskets
and flowers
and songs.
Who cares
about this stuff?
Granny is dead.
She's gone.
She's departed.

Does she care
what color the roses are?

There are three people at our house:
me,
my mom,
and Granny.
And that's how it's always been.
They took her away
when I was at school
and I didn't get to say good-bye.

But she's here.
No longer stuck in her bed,
she fills every room.
I hug her pillow
and breathe in her lavender smell.

I sit on her bench
in the garden
and picture her
pruning the trees.
I stand at the kitchen sink
and see her gloved hands
plunging into the sudsy water.
Then I feel a hand
on my shoulder.
Not Granny.
It's Mom.
Mom, who turns me around,
who pulls me close,
who lets me cry
and cry
and cry,
then makes me milky tea
just like Granny used to.
And tells me
we'll survive.

Mom phones
the school
and says I'll be away
till Monday.
I think of Prudence Jones.
She will be happy
without me there.
Perhaps she can get her
boyfriend back.
I think of Miss Bruff
and her poems.
She will be happy
that I'm not there
to make bad rhymes.
I think of the groups
of sporty boys
and ballet girls
and rough kids.
They will not miss me.
My group of one
will be a group of none.

Mom and Charles talk some more.
And then Mom takes me
to see Father Brierly.
He places his hands on us,
one on Mom's head,
one on mine,
and he prays.
He talks about the funeral.
What hymns did Granny like?
Who will speak of her life?
Then he looks at me.
What about you, Pearl?
Would you like
to say something about your gran?
I shake my head.
No!
I don't want to say good-bye.
I don't want
people staring
while I try to find some words.
I wouldn't know what to say.

Mom frowns.
I am being rude.
But Father Brierly just shrugs.
Perhaps you might change your mind.
No, I say.
I only have one mind.
I'm not going to change it.

Our quiet house
has been invaded.
Old friends,
new friends,
even people I didn't know
were friends,
arrive with flowers,
with cards,
and with food.
Lots of food.
As if lemon cake
or cheese Danish
or shortbread
will fill that empty place
inside us.
Mom smiles
and makes tea
and small talk.

When Miss Bruff comes,
she takes me aside.
We miss you at school, she says.
She gives me a card the class has signed.
Even Prudence Jones.
Mitchell Mason has written
Come back soon.
Perhaps he wants me to write
some more rude poems
about Miss Bruff.
Now Miss Bruff is here
eating lemon cake
with frosting
and saying nice things
to my mom.

Your Pearl, Miss Bruff says,
is a wonderful writer.
She writes the best stories
and essays.
I love to read her work.
But she doesn't like poetry.

Ha!
I say inside my head.
What do you know, Miss Bruff?
I love writing poetry.
You just don't like my style.
You want rhyme
and rhythm
and happy endings,
but my poems
don't rhyme
can't rhyme
shouldn't rhyme.
Rhyme
does not a poem make.

Mom murmurs a sound
of surprise.

I did not know
my Pearl was a writer.
She doesn't show me her stories.
I don't think she showed her granny, either.

Wrong, Mom!
Granny *did* know.
On quiet afternoons
when you were working
and Granny and I were home alone,
I would tell her my stories
and she would tell me hers.

One day Granny read me
a poem
about a man stealing a plum.
Granny, I remember saying,
why are there no rhymes
in that poem?
Granny laughed.
Why, Pearl, didn't you know
a poem does not have to rhyme?
It does not have to be written
in a certain way
at a certain time.
No.
A poem comes
when it is needed
and writes itself
in the way it needs
to get its point across.

I didn't know what
Granny meant
but I knew
that the rhyme could go.

Miss Bruff leaves
and I am glad.
She didn't mean
to upset me
but she did.

In my room
I take a fresh page
and prepare to make my mark.
I will write a poem
without a rhyme in sight
or sound.

I chew my pencil
as I wait for the poem to arrive
and I think of Granny.

Pearl, says Mom,
it is time to get up, darling.
We have to get ready for the funeral.
I yawn and rub my eyes,
pretending I've been asleep.
Really I've been lying awake
most of the night
wondering how
I am going to cope
with saying good-bye
to Granny.
Mom can read my mind.
I know, she says.
It will be hard today.
But maybe Granny
will be there
watching and listening.
Yes, I say.
But I wish she was there
holding my hand, instead.

Churches smell funny
and are mostly old and dusty
but they also feel gentle
and calm.
As we wait to say good-bye,
I wish I was calm inside
but Granny is there
lying in that coffin
all alone.
And outside
Mom and I are now two
instead of the three we've always been.

People who loved Granny
file in behind us
sitting on cold, hard pews
waiting for Father Brierly.
Some look at the coffin,
some look at Mom and me,
and some try
not to look at anything.

In the name of the Father . . .
Father Brierly begins,
and so do my tears.
I do not want to say good-bye to Granny.
I reach into my pocket
for a tissue.
I find two
and give one to Mom.

There are songs
and prayers
and Father Brierly speaks
about what a wonderful lady
Granny was.
He is right, of course
but he did not know Granny
like Mom and me.
At last he stops
and people stand for the final prayer.
But wait.
Someone is walking
to the front of the church.
Someone with red, red eyes
and trembling legs.
That someone is me.
There is something I must do.
I must tell everyone
how much I loved my granny
and I must tell Granny, too.
A piece of paper
is in my hands
and I read:

My granny
Was someone
Who loved
And laughed
And sang
And cared
And cried
And sighed
And shared.
She loved life,
She loved Mom,
And she loved me.
She wasn't here
For long enough,
But I am glad
That she
Was here
At all.

Back in the pew
Mom squeezes my hand
and together we stand
as Granny is wheeled from the church.
But not from our hearts.
We follow her,
the three of us together
for the last time.

Afterward, people want to hug
and kiss
and reassure us,
and we must let them
even if we'd rather
be at home.

How many pieces of cake
can one sad girl eat?
All this food
won't ease the hollow feeling
in my stomach.
Miss Bruff comes empty-handed.
She will not feed me food
but she has words for me.

Pearl, she says,
your poem was beautiful.
Where did you learn
to write like that?

My granny taught me
is all I say.
And I smile at Miss Bruff.

Mom says I must
go back to school.
Back to my group of one
and poems that rhyme
and stealing boyfriends
without meaning to.

It seems I've been away
forever.
The groups are still there
but something is different.
I can't find my group of one.
There is no space for one
when people want to
pat me on the shoulder
and say welcome back.
Perhaps I was never
in a group of one.

Mitchell Mason sits next to me at recess.
Oh, boy.
A boy.
Mitchell, I say,
you are a very nice boy
and you have dreamy eyes.
(Actually I don't say that part—
I just think it to myself.)
But I did not mean to steal you
from Prudence
and I don't need a boyfriend.

Mitchell laughs.
That's a relief.
I don't want a girlfriend, either.
But you are funny
and fun
and I like your poems.
Can I be your friend?
And now I know my group of one
has gone.

At writing time
Miss Bruff stands at the front
and tells us to write a poem.
I sigh
but she smiles at me.
This time, class, she says,
I want a poem that does not rhyme.

But Miss, says Prudence Jones,
a poem must rhyme.
Otherwise it is not a poem.
No, says Miss Bruff.
Sometimes a poem
needs no rhyme
to be just right.
Sometimes a poem
just is.

For a moment
I wonder if Granny
is standing behind Miss Bruff
whispering these thoughts
into her ear.
Thank you, Granny,
I think,
for teaching Miss Bruff
like you taught me.

At home
Mom asks about my day
and I ask about hers.
We sit on the bench that Granny painted
and feel happy-sad
that life goes on.

There are two people
at our house:
Mom
and me.
And somewhere
Granny is watching us —
no longer old
or drooling.
Glad
that we can carry on
without her.